How Big Is God's Love?

Helen Haidle   *Illustrated by*   David Haidle

Harvest House Publishers
Eugene, Oregon 97402

To our fellow Christians

In the Beaverton-Portland area,

Who have reflected God's Love

To us for 27 years.

HOW BIG IS GOD'S LOVE?
Copyright © 1999 David and Helen Haidle
Published by Harvest House Publishers
Eugene, Oregon 97402

Library of Congress Cataloging-in-Publication Data
Haidle, David.
How big is God's love? / David and Helen Haidle.
p. cm.
Summary: Describes God's love as higher and deeper than
anything else found in the whole world.
ISBN 1-56507-927-2
1. God--Love--Juvenile literature. [1. God. 2. Love.]
I. Haidle, Helen. II. Title.
BT140.H34 1998
231'. 6--dc21

Scripture quotations are from The Living Bible, © 1971 owned by assignment by
Illinois Regional Bank N.A. (as trustee). Used by permission of Tyndale House Publishers, Inc,
Wheaton, Illinois 60189.

*M*ay your roots go down deep into the soil of God's marvelous love;

And may you be able to feel and understand, as all God's children should,

How **long**,

how **wide,**

how **deep,**

and how **high** His love really is;

And to experience this love for yourselves, though it is so great that
you will never see the end of it or fully know or understand it.

Ephesians 3:17-19

How big is God's love?
Is it tall as a tree?
Is it deep as the ocean?
Or wide as the sea?

God's love reaches down to each insect and bug;

The cricket and butterfly,

Ant, worm, and slug.

God's love cares for animals—
For puppies and moles;
For gophers and rabbits
Who hide in their holes.

*C*limb up to the top of the tallest of trees,
God's love stretches higher
Than any of these.

Hike up to the rocks where the bald eagles rest.

God's love reaches higher

Than a mountaintop nest.

*L*ike waterfalls ripple
Down the steep mountainside,
God's love overflows to
The world far and wide.

Take a ride in a hot air balloon.
Sail up high!
God's love covers rainbows
And clouds floating by.

*G*od's love circles earth, past the far distant shore.

It's wider than the ocean, whose waves toss and roar.

Dive down to the bottomless depths of the sea;
But you'll never find out how deep
God's love can be.

God's love can't be measured . . .
or counted.
It's more—
Than the small grains of sand
Piled up high on the shore.

God's love wraps around you
And guards you from harm,
Just like Daddy holds you all snug in his arms.

*Explore outer space
With a telescope lens;
You'll never discover where the love of God ends.*

God's love stretches high
   Beyond dark evening skies,
That sparkle with starlight and bright fireflies.

God's love is the greatest.
It's the biggest . . . and BEST!
Now lean back in God's loving arms
As you rest.

Does God Love Me?

Yes! You can be sure that God loves **you** because—
"For God loved the world so much that he gave his only Son
so that anyone who believes in him shall . . . have eternal life."

John 3:16

Look into the Christmas manger
and see God's greatest gift of love.

Jesus grew up and died on the cross
because He loved you.
God brought Jesus back to life.
Now Jesus lives with you every day.
And He will love you forever.